Marjorie Kinnan Rawlings

Writing in Rural Florida

Heather E. Schwartz

Consultants

Dorothy Levin, M.S.Ed., MBA
St. Lucie County Schools

Vanessa Ann Gunther, Ph.D.
Department of History
Chapman University

Cassandra Slone
Pinellas County Public Schools

Publishing Credits

Rachelle Cracchiolo, M.S.Ed., *Publisher*
Conni Medina, M.A.Ed., *Managing Editor*
Emily R. Smith, M.A.Ed., *Series Developer*
Diana Kenney, M.A.Ed., NBCT, *Content Director*
Courtney Patterson, *Multimedia Designer*

Image Credits: Cover and pp.1, 4-5, 9 (bottom), 13 (bottom), 17 (left), 20-21, 29 (bottom) State Archives of Florida; p.4 Historic Florida / Alamy; p.5 MARICE COHN BAND/KRT/Newscom; pp.6 (top, middle, bottom), 12, 15, 16 (left and right), 17 (right), 23 (back), 29 (top) Marjorie Kinnan Rawlings Digital Collections, University of Florida Smathers Libraries; pp.7 (left and right), 32 Public Domain; pp.8-9 Suzanne Tucker / Shutterstock.com; p.9 (top) LOC [LC-USZ62-123458]; p.10-11 LOC [fl0158.photos.052030p]; p.11 (top), 29 (middle) New York Public Library Digital Collections; p.13 (left) Creative Commons Christmas number, Scribner's magazine by Boston Public Library used under CC BY-SA 2.0, (right) Creative Commons Scribner's Magazine, Aug 1916 by tom1231, used under CC BY-SA 2.0; p.18 (bottom) Nagel Photography / Shutterstock.com; p.21 (left) LOC [LC-USZ62-117954], (center) LOC [LC-USZ62-118643], (right) LOC [LC-USZ62-120743]; p.22 Courtesy of Donna Green-Townsend; p.23 (bottom) Pat Canova/Alamy; pp.24, 31 American Library Association (WAITING FOR PERMISSION); p.25 Creative Commons UF00034618 by UF Digital Collections used under CC BY-SA 2.0; pp.24-25 Creative Commons File:Lieber College, University of South Carolina.jpg by Dfscgt21, used under CC0 1.0; p.26 Photo by Alan Anderson. Marjorie Kinnan Rawlings Papers, George A. Smathers Libraries, Univeristy of Florida; p.27 (front) Creative Commons Mkrawlingshouse sign01.jpg by Ebyabe used under CC BY-SA 2.5, (back) Creative Commons Mkrawlingshouse03.jpg by Ebyabe used under CC BY-SA 2.5; all other images from iStock and/or Shutterstock.

Library of Congress Cataloging-in-Publication Data

Names: Schwartz, Heather E., author.
Title: Marjorie Kinnan Rawlings : writing in rural Florida / Heather E. Schwartz.
Description: Huntington Beach, CA : Teacher Created Materials, [2017] |
Includes index.
Identifiers: LCCN 2016014357 (print) | LCCN 2016015183 (ebook) | ISBN
9781493835430 (pbk.) | ISBN 9781480756908 (eBook)
Subjects: LCSH: Rawlings, Marjorie Kinnan, 1896-1953--Juvenile literature. |
Authors, American--20th century--Biography--Juvenile literature. | Country
life--Florida--Juvenile literature.
Classification: LCC PS3535.A845 Z86 2017 (print) | LCC PS3535.A845 (ebook) |
DDC 813/.52 [B] --dc23
LC record available at https://lccn.loc.gov/2016014357

Teacher Created Materials
5301 Oceanus Drive
Huntington Beach, CA 92649-1030
http://www.tcmpub.com

ISBN 978-1-4938-3543-0

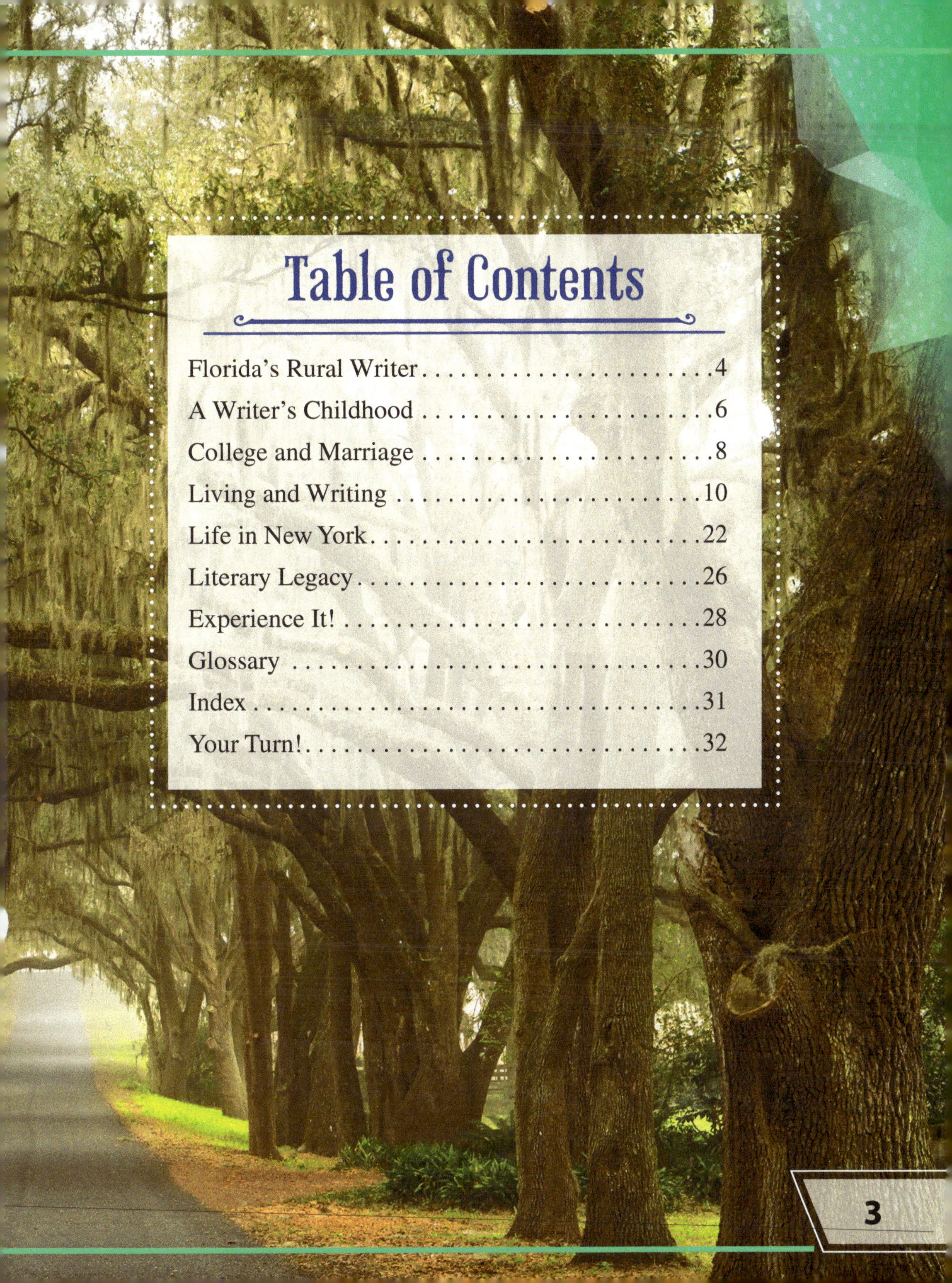

Table of Contents

Florida's Rural Writer

Marjorie Kinnan Rawlings wrote stories, poems, and books during the early- to mid-1900s. Many of her ideas came from her own life experiences. The people she met inspired her. She created characters based on them. She developed plots and themes based on their lives in **rural** areas.

Rawlings chose unique subjects for her writing. Other writers were not writing about these types of people. But, the characters she created were realistic. Readers were drawn to her stories. They liked learning about the people who lived in rural parts of the state.

Marjorie Kinnan Rawlings and her dog

Rawlings loved writing from the time she was a child. But, writing was not easy for her. She often struggled. She might work eight hours to finish only three pages! She had trouble publishing her work, too. At first, many publishers did not like her writing. They did not want to publish it. Rawlings considered quitting after several difficult years. But, she persevered and kept writing.

Finally, Rawlings earned respect as a writer. She grew famous. Her work became her **legacy**. She created literature that would last.

typewriter

A Writer's Childhood

Marjorie Kinnan was born in Washington, DC, on August 8, 1896. Her father was Arthur Frank Kinnan. He was an attorney for the U.S. Patent and Trademark Office. Her mother was Ida May Traphagen. Marjorie had one younger brother named Arthur.

Marjorie grew up on two farms. Her parents had a farm in Maryland. Her grandparents had a farm in Michigan. Marjorie loved farm life. Nature brought her joy.

Arthur Frank Kinnan

Ida May Traphagen

Marjorie as a baby

Marjorie also enjoyed writing. She started writing at the age of six and published some of her work a few years later in the *Washington Post*. She wrote letters and short stories for the newspaper's children's page.

When Marjorie was 16 years old, *McCall's Magazine* held a contest for young writers. She sent in her story "The Reincarnation of Miss Hetty." It won second place and a seventy-five-dollar prize.

But life wasn't full of prizes for Marjorie. Her father died in 1913 when she was only 17 years old. She, her mother, and brother moved soon after. They started a new life in Wisconsin in 1914.

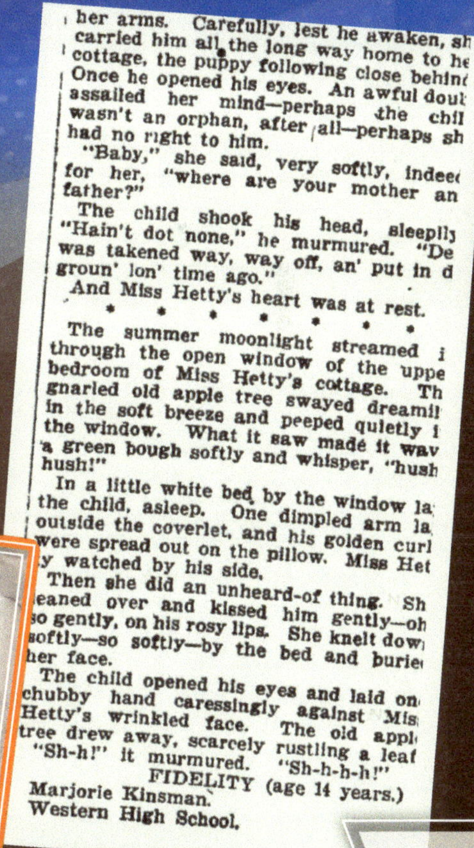

her arms. Carefully, lest he awaken, sh carried him all the long way home to he cottage, the puppy following close behind Once he opened his eyes. An awful dout assailed her mind—perhaps the chil wasn't an orphan, after all—perhaps sh had no right to him.

"Baby," she said, very softly, indeed for her, "where are your mother an father?"

The child shook his head, sleepily "Hain't dot none," he murmured. "De was takened way, way off, an' put in d groun' lon' time ago."

And Miss Hetty's heart was at rest.

* * * * * * *

The summer moonlight streamed i through the open window of the uppe bedroom of Miss Hetty's cottage. Th gnarled old apple tree swayed dreamil in the soft breeze and peeped quietly i the window. What it saw made it wav a green bough softly and whisper, "hush hush!"

In a little white bed by the window la the child, asleep. One dimpled arm la outside the coverlet, and his golden curl were spread out on the pillow. Miss Het y watched by his side.

Then she did an unheard-of thing. Sh eaned over and kissed him gently—oh so gently, on his rosy lips. She knelt dow softly—so softly—by the bed and buried her face.

The child opened his eyes and laid on chubby hand caressingly against Mis Hetty's wrinkled face. The old appl tree drew away, scarcely rustling a leaf "Sh-h!" it murmured. "Sh-h-h-h!"

FIDELITY (age 14 years.)
Marjorie Kinsman.
Western High School.

McCall's Contest

Marjorie's prizewinning story for *McCall's Magazine* was first published in 1911. It appeared in the *Washington Post*. The newspaper misprinted her name as Marjorie Kinsman and said she was 14 years old.

College and Marriage

Marjorie went to the University of Wisconsin after high school. There, she wrote for the college's literary magazine. She also enjoyed drama. She even starred in a play called *Lima Beans.* She graduated from college with honors in 1918.

After college, Marjorie moved to New York. There, she worked for the National Board of the Young Women's Christian Association. She kept writing fiction, too.

In 1919, Marjorie married her college sweetheart, Charles Rawlings. Her name became Rawlings, too. They stayed in New York for a short time. But, they could not find work that they liked. So, they moved to Kentucky. There, she was a writer for the *Louisville Courier-Journal*. Before long, the couple moved back to Rochester. Rawlings quickly found work as a reporter for the *Rochester Evening Journal*.

Rawlings kept writing poems and stories. The journal even gave her a weekly column. The column was called "Songs of the Housewife." She wrote one poem a day, six days a week, for two years.

University of Wisconsin now

University of Wisconsin in 1911

Meeting Charles

Marjorie and Charles met at college. They were classmates. They shared an interest in writing.

Living and Writing

Rawlings needed a change after a few years. She and her husband wanted to spend more time together. She also wanted a peaceful space to write. They decided to move. In 1928, they bought an orange grove near Cross Creek, Florida.

Cross Creek was in a very small, rural town. Rawlings met people who were different from those she knew in New York. They had their own customs and culture. They lived in an area called the **scrub**. They grew crops. They raised **livestock**. They traded with one another for the things they needed. They were perfectly comfortable being isolated from the rest of the state.

Rawlings was inspired by her new surroundings. She wrote about what she saw. She wrote about the people she met. Many white people were **prejudiced** against their black neighbors. Rawlings did not agree with their views. She tried to portray all people honestly and accurately. She did not want to promote **racism**.

Rawlings's house in Cross Creek

Loaded Label

Rawlings wrote stories about Florida Crackers. The term *Cracker* was used to describe southern pioneers who cracked whips to herd cattle. Later, the term described people living in very rural areas of Florida. Today, it is often thought of as a derogatory, or negative, term.

Rawlings catches a crab.

Immersion Journalism

Rawlings used a style of research called *immersion journalism*. Immersion journalism is research in which writers immerse themselves in their topics. They make the topic part of their lives.

Rawlings sold her first story about rural Florida to *Scribner's Magazine* in 1930. The story was called "Cracker Chidlings." It was published in February 1931. But she still wanted to learn more about country life.

As Rawlings spent time living with people in her town, she lived the way they did. She fished. She hunted. She washed large, heavy quilts. She learned to identify plants and animals.

Some of what the people did was against the law. Rawlings hunted deer out of season. She learned to make **moonshine**, an **illegal** home-brewed alcohol. She was not opposed to breaking the law to get a good story. She was fascinated by her neighbors' lifestyle. She felt like she was one of them.

Rawlings's experiences helped her writing. In the past, she was only able to write about the people as an outsider. Now, she knew them personally. She could write about them with sympathy and understanding. This helped her develop more realistic characters. Her writing became more honest.

These men display the fish they caught in the Everglades in the 1930s.

The Great Depression

The Great Depression greatly influenced Rawlings's work. It was a period in the United States that began in 1929 and ended in 1939. Many people were unemployed. They could not support their families.

Unemployed men wait in line at a soup kitchen.

Rawlings used what she learned. She focused her writing. She wrote more about rural Florida. Her experiences helped her form plots. They also helped her create characters. Her writing career took off. Her first book, *South Moon Under*, was published in 1933. It is about a moonshiner's life. Her short story, "Gal Young Un," won the O. Henry Memorial Award the same year. The story is about a woman who marries a con man.

It was a good year. But Rawlings had troubles, too. She enjoyed her new lifestyle, but her husband was not as happy. She and Charles divorced in 1933. Still, Rawlings did not let personal problems stop her. She kept writing. She published *Golden Apples* in 1935.

Rawlings went on to publish *The Yearling* in 1938. This book about a young Florida boy and his adopted fawn won a Pulitzer Prize in 1939. Winning this award sent a strong message to the public. It meant Rawlings was a respected American author.

The Yearling

This is a page from *The Yearling* when it was a work in progress.

Success didn't stop Rawlings. She continued to write. In 1940, she published a book of stories called *When the Whippoorwill*. She published a book called *Cross Creek* two years later.

In *Cross Creek*, Rawlings wrote about her own life. She also wrote about people she knew in rural Florida and their way of life. She wrote about her maid, Idella Parker. She wrote about her friend, Zelma Cason. She also wrote about the Mickens family who were her tenants. She wrote about the lives of the Bass and Glisson families who were her neighbors. She did not aim to flatter her subjects. She tried to be honest. She tried to show them as they were and how she saw them. She tried to represent the truth.

Idella Parker

the Mickens family

Readers wanted more after *Cross Creek* was published. They wanted to make the foods Rawlings described in the book. So, *Cross Creek Cookery* was published in 1942. The cookbook includes Southern dishes and recipes. It also includes stories about the area.

A New Start

In 1941, Rawlings married her second husband, Norton Sanford Baskin. He owned the Castle Warden Hotel in St. Augustine, Florida. Rawlings spent less time at Cross Creek after she remarried.

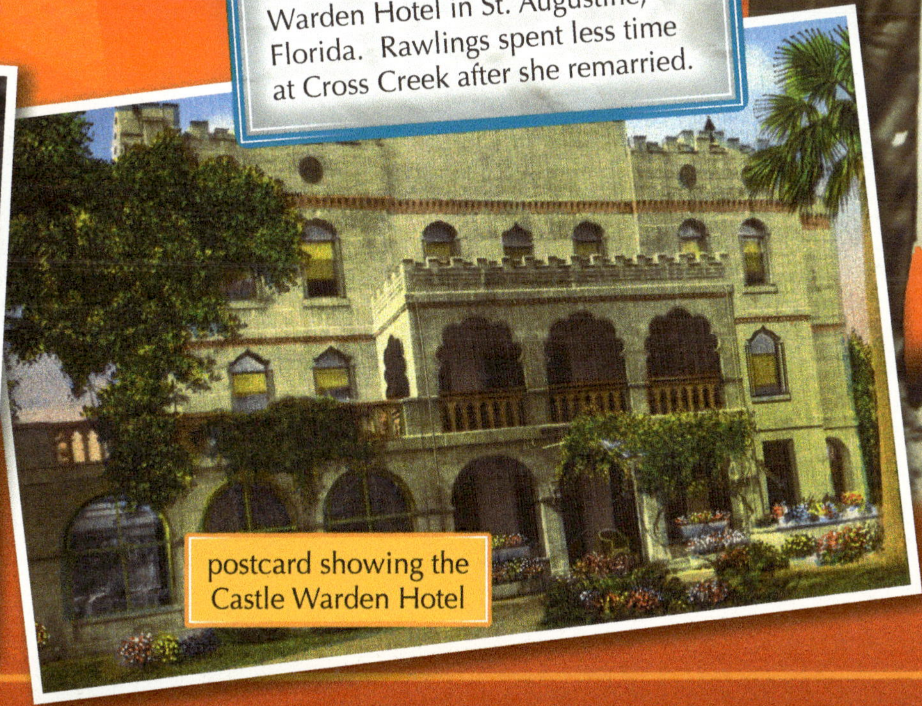

postcard showing the Castle Warden Hotel

Despite the success of *Cross Creek* and *Cross Creek Cookery*, Zelma Cason was not happy. Rawlings's description of Cason may have been accurate, but Cason was upset. Worse than that, she felt her privacy had been invaded. So, she filed a **lawsuit** against Rawlings.

The case against Rawlings was the first of its kind. No one had ever **sued** the author of an **autobiography** for invasion of privacy. The case went to Florida's Supreme Court. It took nearly five years to settle the case. Those years were difficult for Rawlings. The lawsuit took time away from her writing. It used up her energy. She became depressed. In 1948, the case was finally settled—Cason won. The court awarded her one dollar plus court costs. Rawlings had to pay the money.

The lawsuit changed Rawlings as a writer. She only wrote a few more stories and articles set in Cross Creek. Then, she stopped writing about rural Florida. It was time to move on to new subject matter.

Only a Dollar

The judge did not award Cason a big settlement. She proved her privacy had been invaded, but she didn't prove that she'd been harmed. So, the court awarded **nominal damages**, a small symbolic amount.

Florida Supreme Court in Tallahassee, Florida

Rawlings was famous for writing about people and places she knew. She wrote the truth as she saw it. But she had thoughts about other topics, too. She expressed her beliefs about the issues of her time.

The 1940s were a time of change in Florida. People had different opinions about **segregation**. Some people wanted it to continue. They believed in separating the races. Other people wanted to end it. They believed all people should be treated equally.

Bethune leads students from her school in 1904.

Rawlings was against segregation. And she let people know it. She wrote letters to Florida newspapers. She even argued with the state's governor.

Rawlings's friendships reflected her feelings. Her friends included Mary McLeod Bethune and Zora Neale Hurston. Bethune was a black educator and an **activist**. Hurston was a black author. She wrote the classic book *Their Eyes Were Watching God*. Rawlings respected her friends. She believed society should respect them, too.

Famous Friends

Rawlings developed friendships with celebrated authors, such as William Faulkner, Thomas Wolfe, Margaret Mitchell, and Robert Frost. She fished with Ernest Hemingway. She dined with F. Scott Fitzgerald.

William Faulkner

Robert Frost

F. Scott Fitzgerald

Life in New York

Rawlings did not live in Florida full time after the lawsuit. She bought a farmhouse in New York and lived there during the summers. She started writing a new book. She wrote about a man and his family relationships. She set the story in Michigan. It took her many years to complete the book. She was distracted by two major events in her life—her second husband, Norton Sanford Baskin, **enlisted** to fight in World War II, and her trusted editor died. The book was finally published in 1953. It is called *The Sojourner*.

Rawlings wanted to write her next book about a friend named Ellen Glasgow. Glasgow was a fellow author who had died in 1945. Rawlings planned to spend five years researching and writing the biography.

Sadly, Rawlings did not work on it for long. She became ill and had a stroke. She went to a hospital in St. Augustine, Florida. She died in December 1953 at 57 years old. Rawlings is buried in a Florida cemetery.

The Yearling Restaurant

In 1952, a restaurant opened near Rawlings's Florida home. It is named after her book. The restaurant is still open. Its menu features traditional Florida dishes, such as venison, quail, cooter, frog legs, and alligator.

Rawlings left work unfinished when she died. Some of that work was discovered 35 years later. A student at the University of South Carolina was researching Southern female writers. One day, she got a box from a book dealer in New York. It contained old papers. So, she began to read.

The student discovered a manuscript Rawlings had written. It was *Blood of My Blood*. She showed it to other Rawlings fans. They wanted to publish it. First, they had a professional prove the work was really hers. But Rawlings's husband, Norton, did not want the book to be published. He said it belonged to him. The court case that ensued lasted for years. The University Press of Florida was finally allowed to publish the book in 2002 as per Rawlings's will.

Newbery Honor Medal

A children's book, *The Secret River,* was also published after Rawlings's death. It received the Newbery Honor Award in 1956.

University Press of Florida staff discuss their publications.

University of South Carolina

Literary Legacy

When Rawlings moved to Florida in 1928, she chose a life unlike most women in her position. She chose a home on rugged land, away from the city life she was used to. She did not fear or avoid her new neighbors. Instead, she got to know them. She learned their way of life.

She was brave in her personal life when she made these choices. She was brave when she divorced her first husband, for it was not the norm in those days. She was brave in her writing choices, as well. She wrote about subjects that other writers avoided. She wrote what she believed was true, despite the consequences.

Rawlings's legacy lives on through her writing. She leaves behind classics, including *The Yearling* and *Cross Creek*. They provide a record of a particular time and place as well as people of Florida. She paved the way for other women to make brave choices and create important literary works, too.

Open to the Public

The Florida homestead where Rawlings lived and wrote *The Yearling* is now open to the public. It is located in Marjorie Kinnan Rawlings Historic State Park. Visitors can tour her home and farm.

Experience It!

Marjorie Kinnan Rawlings was interested in a specific group of people. She wanted to learn more about them. She did it by living with them. She experienced their lives.

Think about your own interests. Do you dream of singing on stage? Do you wonder what it would be like to work as a veterinarian? What would you like to know more about?

Choose a topic that interests you. Ask your parents to help you find someone who knows about that topic. Interview that person about the topic. Take a tour. Learn all you can.

EVERGLADES

Glossary

activist—a person who uses or supports strong actions, such as protests, to make changes

autobiography—an account of someone's life that is written by that person

enlisted—enrolled in the armed forces

illegal—against the law

lawsuit—a process that involves a court of law resolving a dispute

legacy—something that happened or that comes from someone in the past

livestock—useful farm animals, such as cows, horses, and pigs, that are raised by people

moonshine—a type of alcohol that people make illegally

nominal damages—money awarded to someone who has not suffered injury or loss but whose legal rights were violated

prejudiced—having biased feelings against something or someone

racism—the belief that some races of people are superior over others

rural—relating to the country or area outside a town or city

scrub—land covered with small bushes and trees

segregation—the practice of separating groups of people based on their race or religion

sued—brought a lawsuit against someone

Index

Your Turn!

her arms. Carefully, lest he awaken, sh
carried him all the long way home to he
cottage, the puppy following close behin
Once he opened his eyes. An awful dou
assailed her mind—perhaps the chil
wasn't an orphan, after all—perhaps sh
had no right to him.

"Baby," she said, very softly, indee
for her, "where are your mother an
father?"

The child shook his head, sleepil
"Hain't dot none," he murmured. "De
was takened way, way off, an' put in d
groun' lon' time ago."

And Miss Hetty's heart was at rest.

* * * * * * *

The summer moonlight streamed i
through the open window of the uppe
bedroom of Miss Hetty's cottage. Th
gnarled old apple tree swayed dreamil
in the soft breeze and peeped quietly i
the window. What it saw made it wav
a green bough softly and whisper, "hush
hush!"

In a little white bed by the window la
the child, asleep. One dimpled arm la
outside the coverlet, and his golden curl
were spread out on the pillow. Miss Het
ty watched by his side.

Then she did an unheard-of thing. Sh
leaned over and kissed him gently—oh
so gently, on his rosy lips. She knelt dow
softly—so softly—by the bed and burie
her face.

The child opened his eyes and laid on
chubby hand caressingly against Mis
Hetty's wrinkled face. The old appl
tree drew away, scarcely rustling a leaf
"Sh-h!" it murmured. "Sh-h-h-h!"

FIDELITY (age 14 years.)
Marjorie Kinsman.
Western High School.

A Story of Your Own

Rawlings began writing at an early age. Her story, "The Reincarnation of Miss Hetty," won a prize when she was 16 years old.

Write a story of your own. Decide if it will be fiction or nonfiction. Will you write about people you know? Will the story be set in a familiar town? Share your story with your family and friends.